This Book Belongs To

. . . .

First published in 2001
by Hodder Children's Books

10 9 8 7 6 5 4 3

A Catalogue record for this book is available from the British Library

ISBN 0 340 779365

Printed and bound in Great Britain
by Omnia Books Limited, Glasgow

Hodder Children's Books
A Division of Hodder Headline Limited
338 Euston Road, London NW1 3BH

Fuzzbuzz Takes a Tumble

Written by Margaret Ryan

Illustrated by David Melling

a division of Hodder Headline Limited

To Kirsty and Ivo
with love –
Margaret Ryan

For Igor and Dubravka –
David Melling

Fuzzbuzz, the little orang-utan, was fed up. He wanted his mum to come and play.

"Come and play with me, Mum," he said, and swung round and round her neck.

"Not now, Fuzzbuzz," said his mum. "Can't you see I'm busy chatting?"

But Fuzzbuzz was still fed up.

"Come and play with me, Mum," he said again, and jumped up and down on her back.

"Not now, Fuzzbuzz," said his mum. "Can't you see I'm busy eating?"

But Fuzzbuzz was still fed up.

“Come and play with me, Mum,” he said one more time, and stuck his fingers in her ears.

"Pardon? What did you say?" said his mum. "I can't hear you."

By this time Fuzzbuzz was really fed up.

“I’m going to find my jungle friends,” he said. “THEY’LL play with me.” And he swung away through the trees.

“I’ll look for Bumpy, first,”
he said. “She’s usually up in the
trees eating honey.”

Fuzzbuzz swung on and on through the trees. Bumpy, the sun bear, wasn't there. But the monkeys were.

“Have any
of you seen
Bumpy?”
asked Fuzzbuzz,
and swung
round and
round on the
monkeys’ tails.

The monkeys were
not very pleased
to see him.

They screeched . . .

"GO AWAY, GO AWAY,
BUMPY BEAR'S
NOT HERE TODAY."

"Okay, okay. Keep your tails on," giggled Fuzzbuzz, and went on his way.

Then he wondered who to look for next.

"I know," he said. "I'll look for Smiler. He's usually in the river, having a snooze."

Fuzzbuzz splish splashed into the river. Smiler, the crocodile, wasn't there. But the elephants were.

"Have any of you seen Smiler?" he shouted and jumped up and down on the elephants' backs.

The elephants were not very pleased to see him.

They trumpeted . . .

"GO AWAY, GO AWAY,
SMILER CROC'S
NOT HERE TODAY."

"Okay, okay. Keep your trunks on," said Fuzzbuzz, and went on his way.

Then he wondered who to look for next.

"I know," he said. "I'll look for Rainbow. She's usually in the bat cave having a chat."

Fuzzbuzz tiptoed into the bat cave. Rainbow, the parrot, wasn't there. But the sleeping bats were.

"Have any of you seen Rainbow?" he yelled, and woke them all up.

The bats were not very pleased to see him.

They squeaked . . .

"GO AWAY, GO AWAY,
RAINBOW BIRD'S
NOT HERE TODAY."

"Okay, okay. Keep your ears on," yawned Fuzzbuzz, and went on his way.

By this time he was getting
very tired.
“Time for a little sleep,” he said.
“I’ll make a bed up in the trees
just like Mum showed me.”

He gathered branches, twigs and
leaves and made a bed.

"That looks about right,"
he yawned.

He jumped on to the bed.

He fell right through it.
Right on to the ground.
Right on to his head.

"Ow," he yelled, giving his head a rub. "That hurt."

Along the riverbank Smiler heard the noise.

"What's up, Fuzzbuzz?" he called.

"I fell through my bed right on to my head," said Fuzzbuzz. "And I'm tired and I want to go to sleep."

Smiler thought for a moment.
"Why not sleep in the old boat along the river?" he said.

"Good idea," said Fuzzbuzz, and hitched a ride on Smiler's back.

Soon they came to the old boat.

Fuzzbuzz jumped off Smiler's back into it.

CRASH BANG WALLOP!

He fell right through it.
Right on to the river-bed.
Right on to his bottom.

"Ow," he yelled, giving his bottom a rub. "That hurt."

Deep in the bushes Rainbow heard the noise.

"What's up, Fuzzbuzz?"
she called.

"I fell through my bed right on to my head. I fell through this old boat right on to my bottom. I'm tired and I want to go to sleep," wailed Fuzzbuzz.

Rainbow thought for a moment.
"Why not sleep in the big hollow tree over there?" she said.

"Good idea," said Fuzzbuzz, and followed Rainbow to the big hollow tree.

"This looks great," said Fuzzbuzz, and climbed in.

He fell right down inside it.
Right to the bottom of the tree.
Right on to his chin.

"Ow," he yelled, giving his chin a rub. "That hurt."

Up in the trees Bumpy heard the noise. She bumped down to the ground.

"What's up, Fuzzbuzz?"
she asked.

"I fell through my bed right
on to my head. I fell through the
old boat right on to my bottom.
I fell down the big hollow tree
right on to my chin. And I'm
tired and I want to go to sleep,"
wailed Fuzzbuzz.

"What a shame," said Bumpy. "I'll help you look for somewhere to sleep if you'll help me look for some honey."

"I'm sure I saw some bees in the trees over there," said Fuzzbuzz.
"Let's go and look," said Bumpy.

Up and up and up they climbed.
Then up and up and up
some more.

"Yummy yum yum," said Bumpy when she found the honey.

She was just reaching for it when . . . **RRRIIIPPP!** her claws skidded on the bark. "HELP!" she cried, and grabbed hold of Fuzzbuzz.

"Ow," yelled Fuzzbuzz.

He fell down on to the ground.
Right on to his nose.
Right into the middle of the
Angry Ant Gang.

They were very pleased to see him. They chanted . . .

"WE'RE LEAN, WE'RE MEAN,
WE'RE VERY VERY KEEN
TO STING ANY BIT OF YOU
THAT CAN BE SEEN!"

And they stung his chin,
his bottom and his head.

Fuzzbuzz tried to rub all the sore bits at once. **"Ow, ow, ow,"** he yelled. "That really hurt. I want my mum."

Up in a tall tree his mum heard the noise.

She hurried to find Fuzzbuzz. "Where have you *been*, Fuzzbuzz?" she said. "I've been looking for you everywhere.

"Don't you know it's past your bedtime?"

But Fuzzbuzz didn't reply. He had jumped on to his mum's back and was already fast asleep.